THOMAS & FRIENDS™

THE WAY LITTLE ENGINES WORK

- HOW THEY RUN
- HOW THEY'RE FIXED
- HOW THEY'RE BUILT

Random House 🏠 New York

Illustrations by John Lawson: pages 8–25, 30–33
All illustrations © 2009 Gullane (Thomas) LLC

Thomas the Tank Engine & Friends™

CREATED BY BRITT ALLCROFT

Based on the Railway Series by the Reverend W Awdry
© 2009, 2017 Gullane (Thomas) LLC
Thomas the Tank Engine & Friends and Thomas & Friends
are trademarks of Gullane (Thomas) LLC. Thomas the Tank
Engine & Friends and Design Is Reg. U.S. Pat. & Tm. Off.
© 2017 HIT Entertainment Limited.
All rights reserved. Published in the United States by
Random House Children's Books, a division of Penguin
Random House LLC, 1745 Broadway, New York, NY 10019,
and in Canada by Penguin Random House Canada Limited,
Toronto. Originally published in hardcover and in different
form as *Thomas the Tank Engine Owners' Workshop Manual*
by Haynes Publishing, by arrangement with Egmont UK,
in Great Britain, in 2009 and reissued in paperback in 2015.
Random House and the colophon are registered trademarks
of Penguin Random House LLC.

ISBN 978-1-5247-2075-9

rhcbooks.com   www.thomasandfriends.com

Printed in the United States of America

10 9 8 7 6 5 4 3 2 1

Random House Children's Books supports the First Amendment and
celebrates the right to read.

HiT entertainment

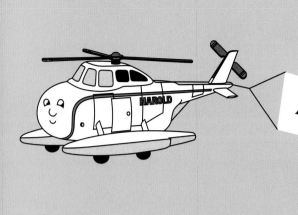

AUTHOR: CHRIS OXLADE

CONTENTS

WELCOME ABOARD!

Welcome to *The Way Little Engines Work*!

And hello from Thomas and his friends.

This book is all about Thomas and the other engines that work on the Island of Sodor.

● REALLY USEFUL FACT ●

Watch for *Really Useful Fact* boxes filled with fantastic Thomas facts.

STATION

THOMAS THE TANK ENGINE

Thomas has water tanks on each side of his boiler. That's why he is called Thomas the Tank Engine!

Thomas pulls his carriages, Annie and Clarabel, and freight trucks.

Thomas has six wheels.

Funnel

Dome

Smoke box

Boiler

Brake pipe

Coupling for pulling trucks and carriages

Buffers for pushing trucks and carriages

Coupling hook

Lamp rod

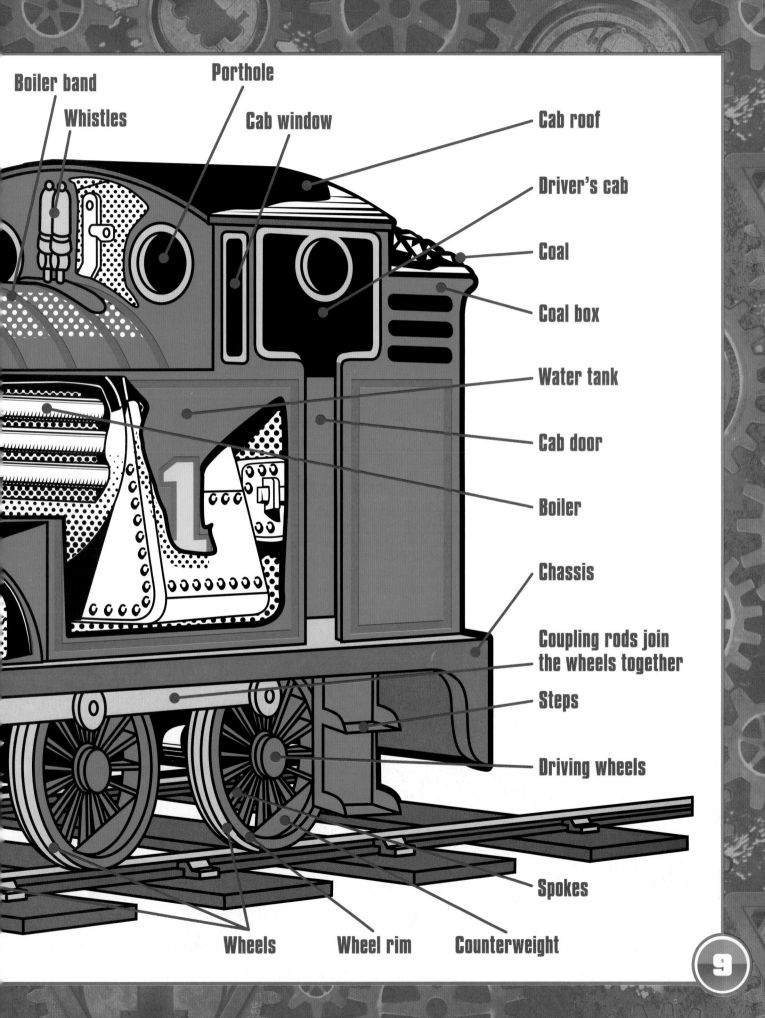

Boiler band

Whistles

Porthole

Cab window

Cab roof

Driver's cab

Coal

Coal box

Water tank

Cab door

Boiler

Chassis

Coupling rods join the wheels together

Steps

Driving wheels

Spokes

Wheels

Wheel rim

Counterweight

9

The Fireman starts a fire in Thomas' firebox. He shovels in coal to make the fire burn fiercely. The fire boils water in the boiler to make steam.

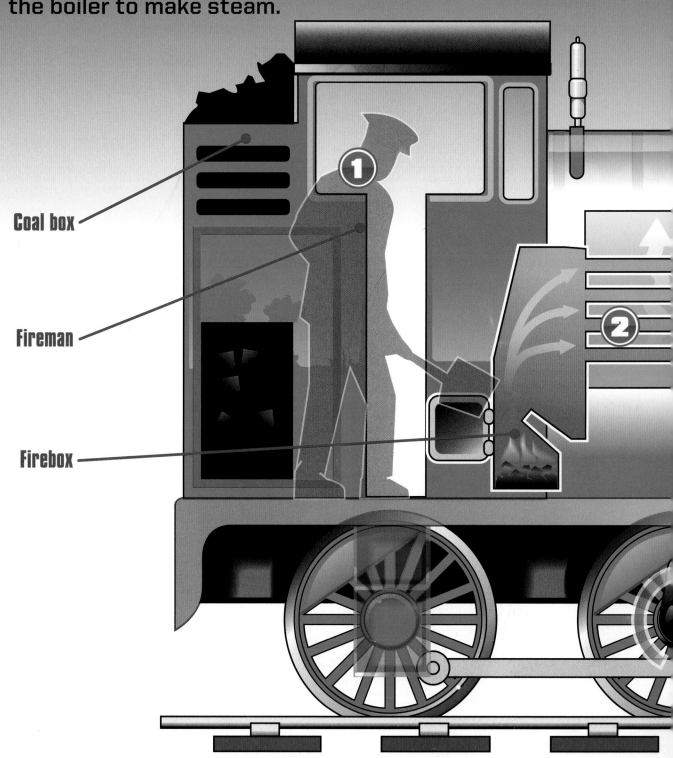

Coal box

Fireman

Firebox

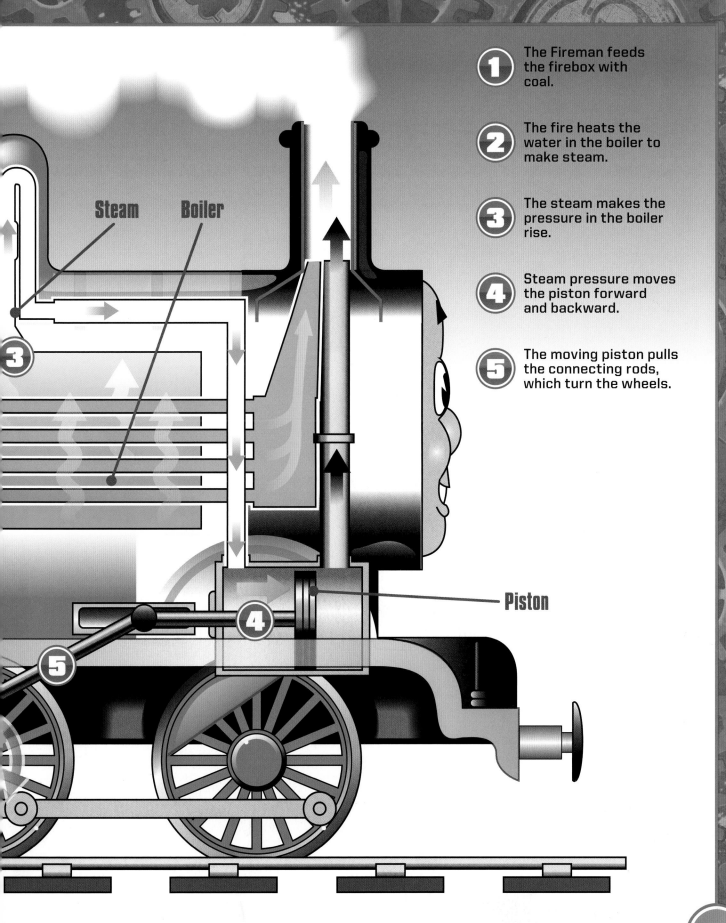

1 The Fireman feeds the firebox with coal.

2 The fire heats the water in the boiler to make steam.

3 The steam makes the pressure in the boiler rise.

4 Steam pressure moves the piston forward and backward.

5 The moving piston pulls the connecting rods, which turn the wheels.

Steam   Boiler

Piston

Thomas the Tank Engine has two crew members.

His Driver makes him speed up and slow down, and go forward and backward.

His Fireman looks after his fire and boiler.

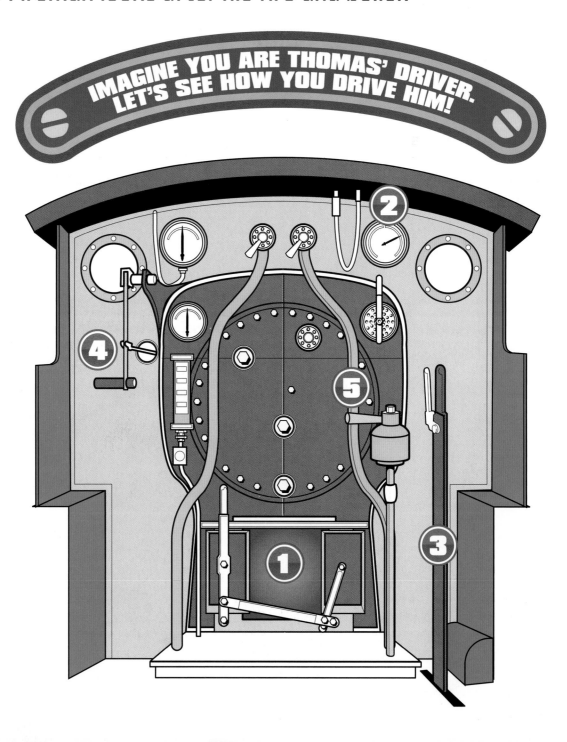

IMAGINE YOU ARE THOMAS' DRIVER. LET'S SEE HOW YOU DRIVE HIM!

1 The Fireman starts a fire in Thomas' firebox. He shovels in coal to make the fire burn fiercely. The fire boils water in the boiler to make steam.

2 Pull on the handle to make Thomas' whistle peep. The whistle warns people that Thomas is ready to move.

3 There is a long pole coming up from the floor. It is called the reverser handle. Push it forward.

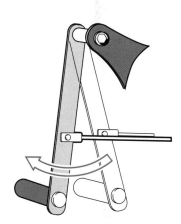

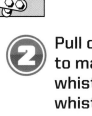

4 There is a long rod high up in front of you. This is the regulator. Pull it out to make steam rush into the cylinders. You can hear the *chuff*, *chuff* of the steam in the funnel. We're off!

5 We're coming to a station. Time to stop! Push the regulator forward. Now turn the brake levers to work the brakes and make Thomas slow down.

Thomas needs some more water. Stop at the water tower. The Fireman puts the hose into Thomas' water tanks.

Gordon is the fastest and most powerful engine on Sodor's railways. He pulls the passenger Express train.

Gordon is a tender engine. He pulls a tender with coal and water for his fire and boiler.

Gordon has twelve wheels. His tender has six wheels.

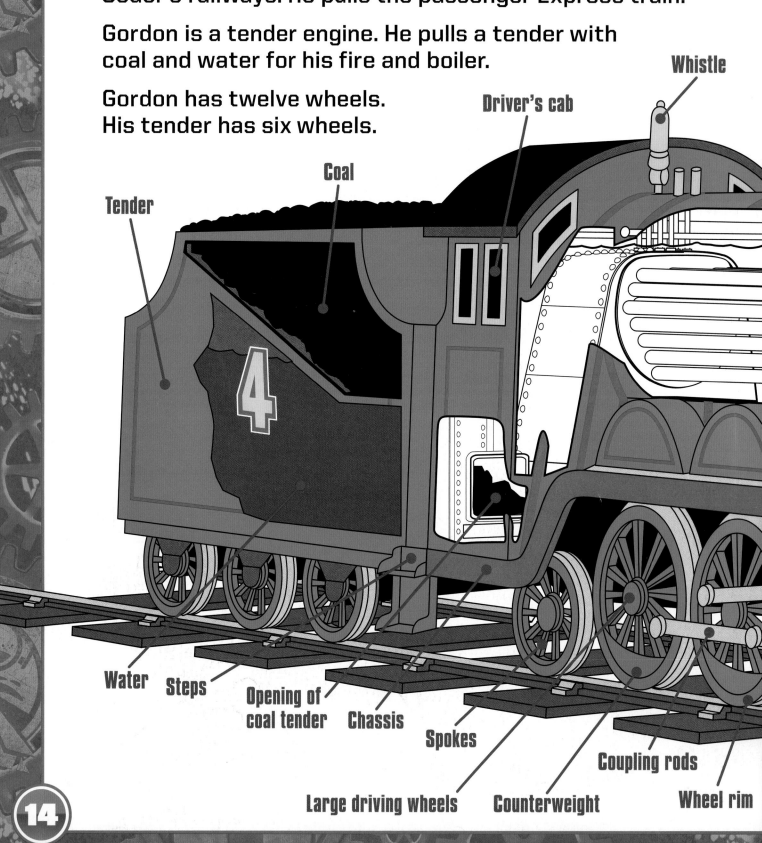

Whistle

Driver's cab

Coal

Tender

Water   Steps

Opening of coal tender   Chassis

Spokes

Large driving wheels   Counterweight

Coupling rods

Wheel rim

Steam dome

Boiler

Funnel

Coupling for
pulling carriages

Buffers for
pushing carriages

Lamp rods

Brake pipe

Piston

15

The engines of Sodor are looked after carefully to keep them working. They are cleaned every day, and if something goes wrong, they visit the engine repair shed to be fixed.

The Drivers and Firemen polish and wipe pipes and paintwork to keep them gleaming.

Engineers check that all the parts are working properly. They tighten any loose nuts and bolts. They squirt on oil and grease to keep everything moving smoothly. Oil makes the wheels turn easily.

Thomas and the other engines work hard. Sometimes their parts wear out or break. Engineers take off the worn-out or broken parts and replace them with new ones.

Every few years the engines are overhauled. That means they get new parts and a fresh coat of paint to make them look clean and new.

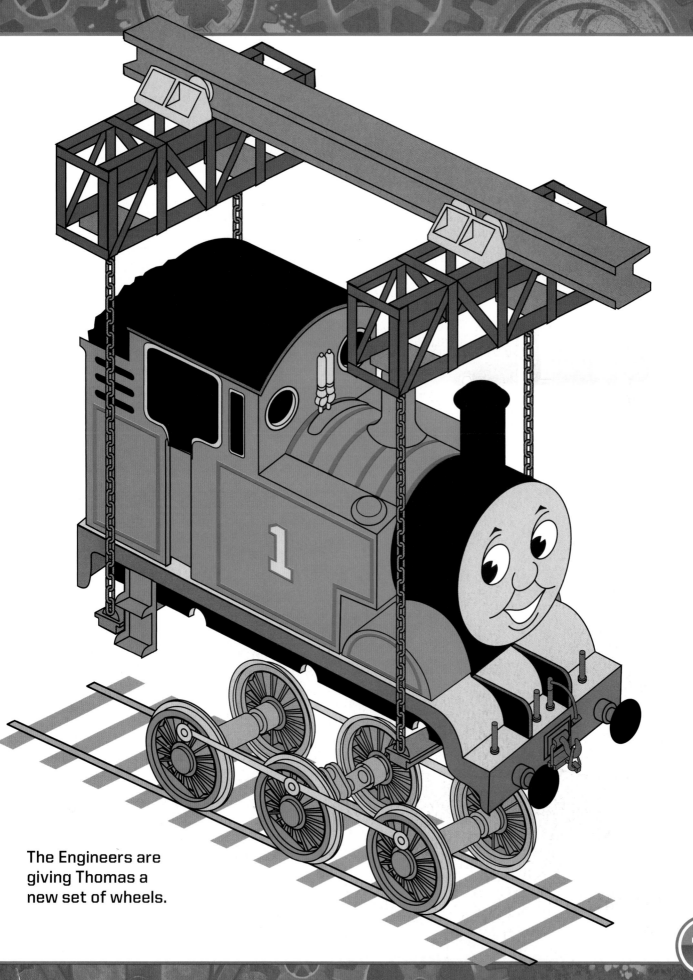

The Engineers are
giving Thomas a
new set of wheels.

Henry is a hardworking engine who pulls coaches and trucks. But he wasn't always so Useful. Here's the story of how Henry changed.

Henry was built as an experiment. His firebox wasn't big enough. So when he arrived on Sodor, he could not make enough steam to go fast or pull heavy loads.

Henry's old firebox

One snowy night Henry was pulling the *Flying Kipper*. He went over some frozen points that sent him into a siding at high speed. He crashed into another train and was badly damaged.

Henry was sent to the Mainland to a big engine repair shed at Crewe. He was repaired, and Sir Topham Hatt decided to give him a new, bigger firebox, too.

Henry's new firebox

When Henry got home, everybody was excited to see his new firebox. Now Henry has no problem making lots of steam.

◦ REALLY USEFUL FACT ◦

Henry was first painted green, but was repainted blue as a reward for helping Edward pull Gordon's Express train. Later he was repainted green again, and he has been green ever since.

PERCY

Percy is a small engine who often works in the quarries and mines on the Island.

Percy is a saddle-tank engine. His water tank sits around his boiler, like the saddle on a horse.

He has four big wheels.

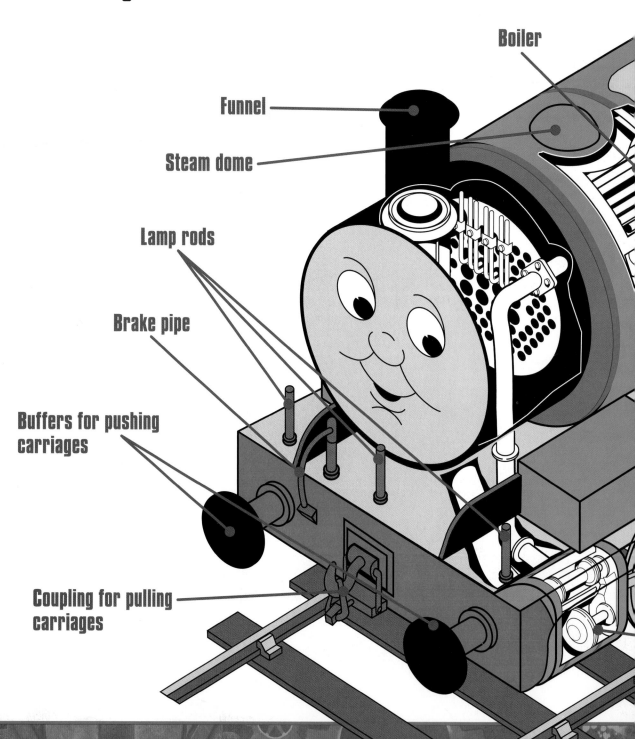

Boiler

Funnel

Steam dome

Lamp rods

Brake pipe

Buffers for pushing carriages

Coupling for pulling carriages

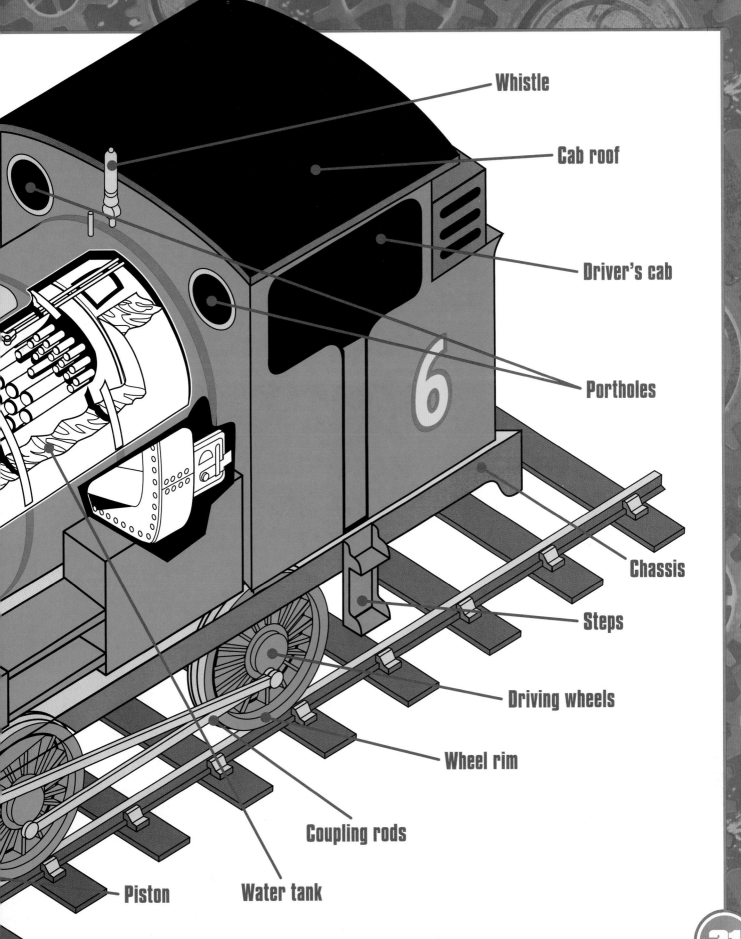

Whistle

Cab roof

Driver's cab

Portholes

6

Chassis

Steps

Driving wheels

Wheel rim

Coupling rods

Piston   Water tank

BUILDING AN ENGINE

Follow these steps to see how an engine is made. The metal pieces are made and joined together in a huge factory.

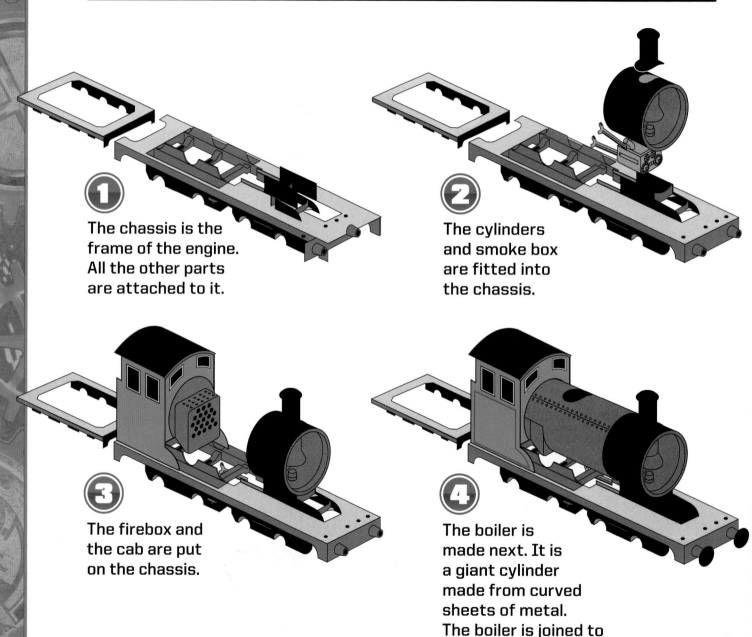

1 The chassis is the frame of the engine. All the other parts are attached to it.

2 The cylinders and smoke box are fitted into the chassis.

3 The firebox and the cab are put on the chassis.

4 The boiler is made next. It is a giant cylinder made from curved sheets of metal. The boiler is joined to the chassis.

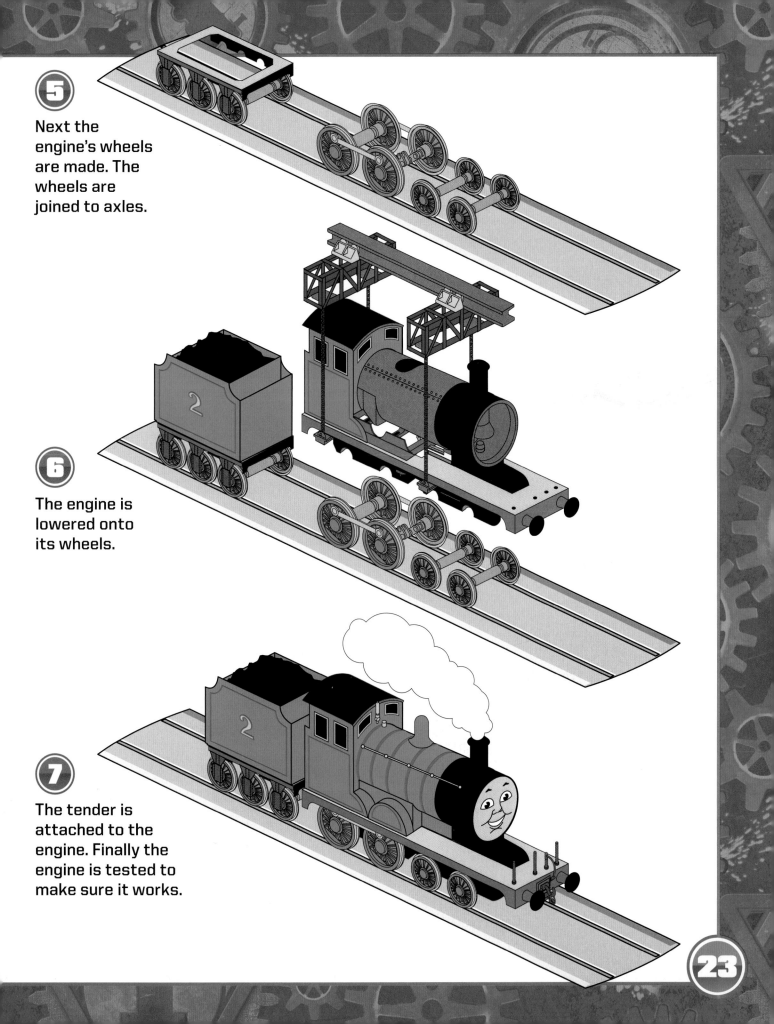

5 Next the engine's wheels are made. The wheels are joined to axles.

6 The engine is lowered onto its wheels.

7 The tender is attached to the engine. Finally the engine is tested to make sure it works.

Mavis is not a steam engine. She has a powerful diesel engine inside that makes her move.

Mavis is a shunting engine. She works hard at the quarry, where she pushes and pulls trucks and carriages.

Mavis has six wheels, which are joined together to help her move heavy loads.

Mavis has a cowcatcher. She uses it to gently push cows off the track when they get in the way.

Buffers for shunting

Cowcatcher

Lamp rods

Coupling

Brake pipe

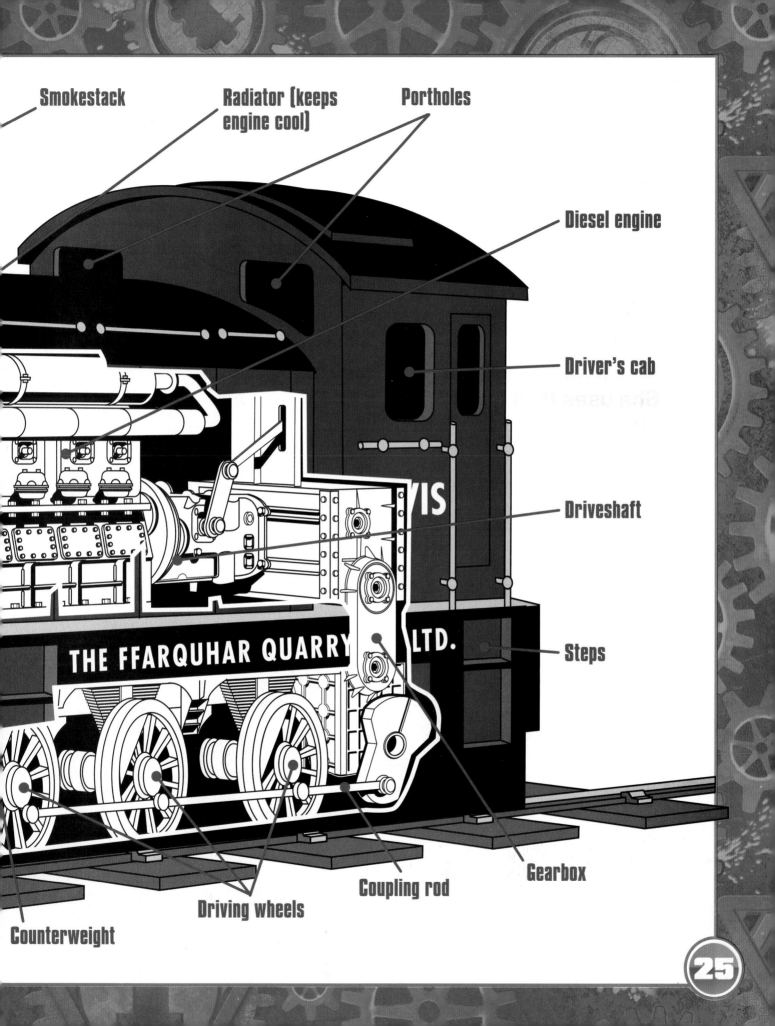

Smokestack

Radiator (keeps engine cool)

Portholes

Diesel engine

Driver's cab

Driveshaft

Steps

THE FFARQUHAR QUARRY LTD.

Gearbox

Coupling rod

Driving wheels

Counterweight

LOTS MORE ENGINES

Let's find out about some of Thomas' friends on Sodor. They come in all shapes and sizes.

EDWARD
ENGINE NUMBER 2
NUMBER OF WHEELS 8
Edward is a tender engine. He pulls coaches and trucks.

◎ REALLY USEFUL FACT ◎

Edward and James are tender engines. Each one pulls a tender that is full of water for his boiler and coal for his fire.

JAMES
ENGINE NUMBER 5
NUMBER OF WHEELS 8
James is a tender engine. He pulls coaches and trucks.

GORDON
ENGINE NUMBER 4   NUMBER OF WHEELS 12
Gordon is a big tender engine. He is the fastest engine on Sodor. He pulls the Express train.

◎ REALLY USEFUL FACT ◎

Percy is a saddle-tank engine. Saddle-tank engines have a tank for water that fits over their boilers.

PERCY
ENGINE NUMBER 6
NUMBER OF WHEELS 4
Percy is a saddle-tank engine. He pulls coaches and trucks.

HENRY
ENGINE NUMBER 3
NUMBER OF WHEELS 10
Henry is a tender engine. He pulls coaches and trucks.

MAVIS
NUMBER OF WHEELS 6
Mavis is a diesel engine. She works at the Ffarquhar Quarry, shunting trucks loaded with stone.

TOBY
ENGINE NUMBER 7
NUMBER OF WHEELS 6
Toby is a steam tram engine. He works on a quarry line and on Thomas' Branch Line.

Not all of Thomas' friends live on Sodor's railways.

ANNIE AND CLARABEL
Annie and Clarabel are Thomas' passenger carriages.

CRANKY THE CRANE
Cranky works at the docks, lifting cargo between ships and trains.

⚬ REALLY USEFUL FACT ⚬

Lots of Troublesome Trucks work at the Ffarquhar Quarry. They carry heavy loads of stone.

TROUBLESOME TRUCKS
The trucks carry all sorts of cargo on Sodor's railways. They work all over the Island. They love to cause trouble!

ROCKY

Rocky is a special truck with a strong crane for lifting engines back onto the track.

ALFIE THE DIGGER

Alfie is a digger who loves working hard and getting dirty.

BERTIE THE BUS

Bertie is a single-decker bus. He carries passengers along the roads of Sodor.

TREVOR

Trevor is a traction engine. He's like a farm tractor, but he is also a steam engine, like Thomas.

Trevor works in the Vicarage Orchard, where he pulls trailers of fruit and sometimes gives children rides.

Trevor has wide metal wheels that grip the ground and keep him from sinking into the mud.

His steam engine turns a heavy flywheel, which turns his wheels.

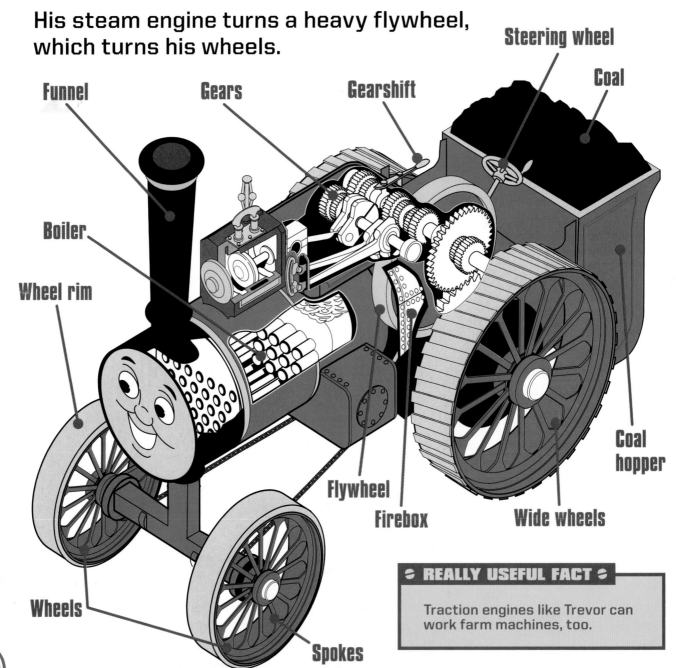

Funnel

Gears

Gearshift

Steering wheel

Coal

Boiler

Wheel rim

Flywheel

Firebox

Wide wheels

Coal hopper

Wheels

Spokes

◦ REALLY USEFUL FACT ◦

Traction engines like Trevor can work farm machines, too.

Harold is a helicopter, who is often seen flying over Sodor.

Harold's main rotor spins around very fast. When it's spinning, it lifts Harold into the air.

Harold has floats for landing on water and wheels for landing on the ground.

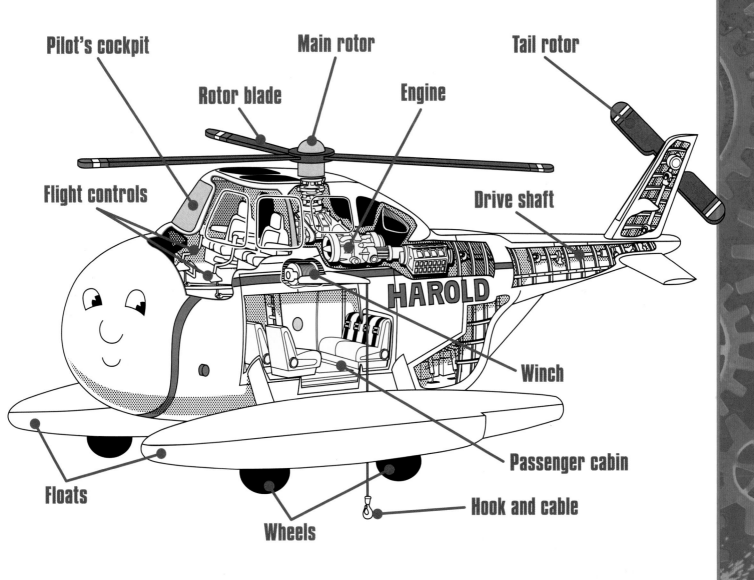

Pilot's cockpit

Main rotor

Tail rotor

Rotor blade

Engine

Flight controls

Drive shaft

HAROLD

Winch

Floats

Passenger cabin

Wheels

Hook and cable

⚙ REALLY USEFUL FACT ⚙

Thomas and the other engines call Harold "Whirlybird" because his rotors whirl around.

THE TRACKS OF SODOR

Sodor has lots of railway lines. The Main Line goes from one side of the Island to the other. Branch Lines lead from the Main Line into the countryside and to the coast.

TRACKS

Railway tracks have two strong metal rails. The rails rest on thick planks of wood called sleepers. Under the sleepers are stones called ballast.

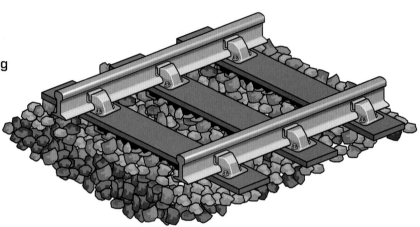

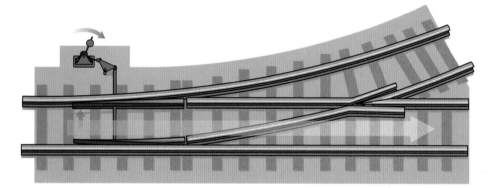

POINTS

Points let trains turn off one track onto another. You see lots of points at stations, where branch lines leave the main line, and in sidings.

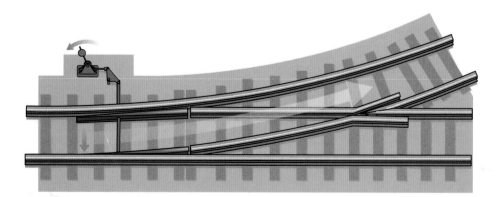

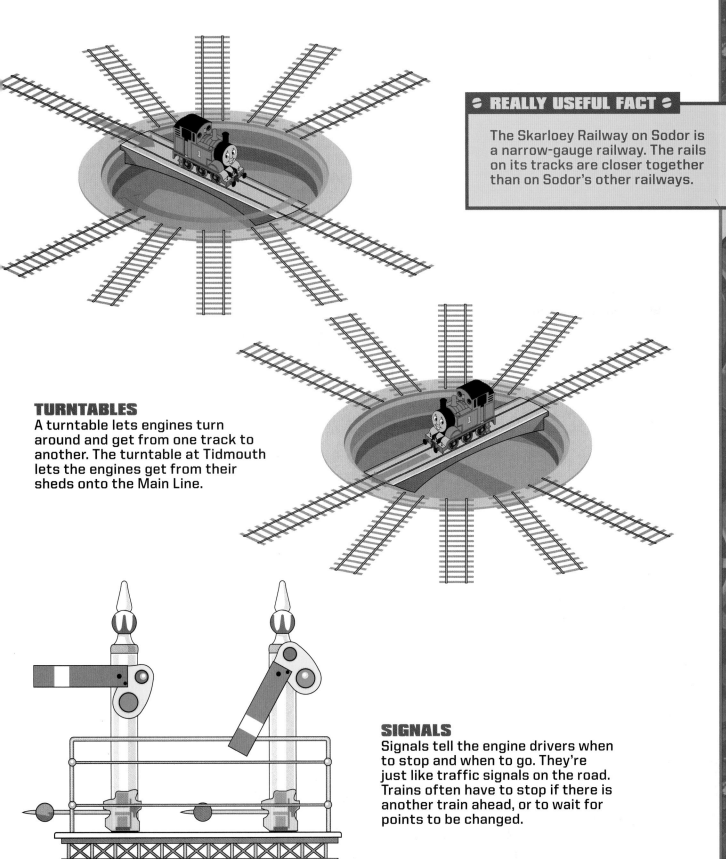

TURNTABLES

A turntable lets engines turn around and get from one track to another. The turntable at Tidmouth lets the engines get from their sheds onto the Main Line.

SIGNALS

Signals tell the engine drivers when to stop and when to go. They're just like traffic signals on the road. Trains often have to stop if there is another train ahead, or to wait for points to be changed.

THIS MEANS STOP. THIS MEANS GO.

OLD AND NEW ENGINES

There are lots of different engines on Sodor's railways. Some are old and some are new. Here you can see what trains from the past and modern trains look like.

THE FIRST STEAM ENGINES
The first railway engines were made more than 200 years ago. They are very old and don't work anymore.

NARROW-GAUGE ENGINES
Narrow-gauge engines like Freddie were built about 200 years ago. They were very slow.

FREDDIE 7

⊙ REALLY USEFUL FACT ⊙

Today the fastest trains are electric trains. They have big electric motors that turn their wheels. There are no electric trains on Sodor.

THE FIRST EXPRESS TRAINS

Engines like Emily were made about 100 years ago. Emily was built to pull Express trains. She has two large driving wheels.

NEWER STEAM ENGINES

Later steam engines were big, fast, and powerful, like Spencer. He has a smooth body to help him whizz along the tracks.

SPENCER

DIESEL ENGINES

Diesel engines are modern engines. They have diesel engines, like those in a large car or truck, but much bigger and more powerful.

THOMAS' RAILWAY FACTS

Chuff, chuff! The noise of steam engines is made by steam coming out of their funnels.

Thomas works on his own Branch Line. It runs between Tidmouth and the town of Ffarquhar.

Shunting engines, such as Mavis and Bert, work in the sidings. They push, pull, and sort wagons.

Thomas' whistle works by steam. When his Driver pulls a string, steam rushes through the whistle.

Sodor is an island. But the Main Line is connected to the Mainland. That's how Henry got to Crewe to be repaired.

Clackety-clack, clackety-clack! That's the noise of Thomas' wheels going over joints in the rails.

The Culdee Fell Railway is very steep. It has a special extra rail that the trains hold on to to stop them from sliding down.

What are those black towers beside the track? They are water towers, holding big tanks of water for the engines.

The steam engines use up water in their boilers as they work. They often stop at water towers to refill their water tanks.

Harvey is a crane engine. If an engine comes off the rails, Harvey helps to lift it back on again.

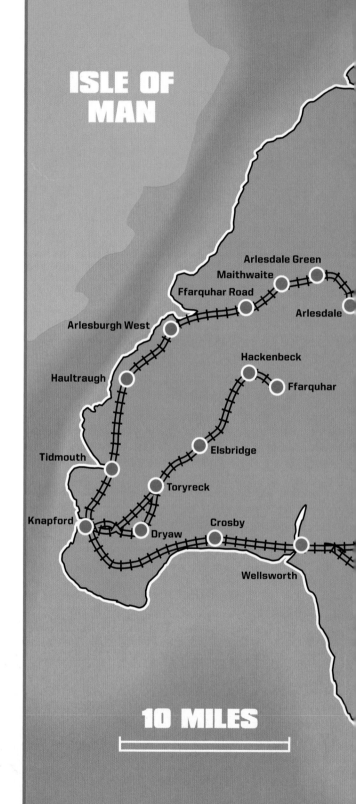

ISLE OF MAN

Arlesdale Green
Maithwaite
Ffarquhar Road
Arlesburgh West
Arlesdale
Hackenbeck
Haultraugh
Ffarquhar
Elsbridge
Tidmouth
Toryreck
Knapford
Crosby
Dryaw
Wellsworth

10 MILES

SODOR

ENGLAND

Culdee Fell Summit

Skarloey Road

Shilah

Kirk Machan

Rheneas

Skarloey

Glennock

Abbey

Cronk

Kildane

Maron

Cros-ny-Cuirn

Crovan's Gate

Suddery

Kellsthorpe Road

Rolf's Castle

Brendam

Kirk Ronan

Barrow

Vicarstown

Ballahoo

Norramby

THOMAS' REALLY USEFUL WORDS

BOILER
Part of a steam engine. This is where water is heated to make the steam that moves the engine's wheels.

CHASSIS
Part of a steam engine. It is a strong frame to which all the engine's other parts are attached.

COUPLING
A hook and chain used to join engines, carriages, and trucks to each other.

DIESEL ENGINE
A railway engine with a big diesel engine that moves it along.

FREIGHT
Anything carried by railway trucks, such as packages, wood, coal, or ballast.

BRANCH LINE
A railway line that connects stations on the main line to other stations.

BUFFERS
Every railway engine, carriage, and truck has buffers at each end. They stop the engines, carriages, and trucks from bumping into each other.

CYLINDER
Part of a steam engine. Steam goes into the cylinder and pushes a piston backward and forward.

PISTON
Part of a steam engine that makes the wheels turn. Steam pushes it backward and forward inside the engine's cylinders.

QUARRY
A place where rocks are dug out of the ground.

WATER TANK
A container on a steam engine that stores water for the boiler.

SIDINGS
Railway tracks where carriages and trucks are stored when they are not being used.

TENDER ENGINE
A steam engine that pulls a tender behind it. The tender is full of coal and water.

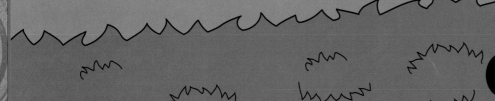

FIREBOX
Part of a steam engine. This is where the fire burns to heat the water in the boiler.

SADDLE TANK
A water tank that sits over the top of a steam engine's boiler. An engine with a saddle tank is called a saddle-tank engine.

FUNNEL
A chimney on top of a steam engine where smoke and steam come out.

NARROW GAUGE
A railway with rails that are close to each other. On Sodor, the Skarloey Railway is a narrow-gauge railway.

In the early 1940s, a loving father crafted a small blue wooden engine for his son, Christopher. The stories this father, the Reverend W Awdry, made up to accompany the wonderful toy were first published in 1945. Reverend Awdry continued to create new adventures and characters until 1972, when he retired from writing.